HOW I SAVED HANUKKAH

• • • • • • • • • • • ◆ • • • • • • • • • •

HOW I SAVED HANUKKAH

Amy Goldman Koss

pictures by Diane deGroat

SCHOLASTIC INC.

New York   Toronto   London   Auckland   Sydney
Mexico City   New Delhi   Hong Kong   Buenos Aires

ISBN 0-439-35644-X

Text copyright ©1998 by Amy Goldman Koss. Pictures copyright
©1998 by Diane deGroat. All rights reserved.
Published by Scholastic Inc., 555 Broadway, New York, NY 10012,
by arrangement with Dial Books for Young Readers, a divison of Penguin Putnam
Inc. SCHOLASTIC and associated logos are trademarks and/or
registered trademarks of Scholastic Inc.

12 11 10 9 8 7 6 5 4 3 2 1   1 2 3 4 5 6/0

Printed in the U.S.A.   40

First Scholastic printing, November 2001

Designed by Julie Rauer

Thanks to Sandy Medof, Sue Horton, Jim White, and Cindy Kane.

Kisses to: Momba, Poppa Bear, Emily, Bennett, and my Freen. Happy Hanukkah! A.G.K.

• • • • • • • • • • • ◆ • • • • • • • • • •

CHAPTER

• • • • • • • • • I • • • • • • • •

"**W**e shouldn't have to come to school when there's a sub," my best friend, Lucy, was saying. "When the teacher stays home, we should too."

I nodded and said, "I was just thinking that the last few days of school before the holiday recess are such a waste, they should just cancel them. We'd start vacation the week before. But then *that* week would be the last week before vacation so *it* would be useless, and might as well be canceled."

"We could cancel backward all the way to the first day of school," Lucy said. "And since we know the first day is worthless, we might as well skip it too. Right?"

That's why Lucy Doyle is my best friend. Not only does she understand me, she also agrees with me.

"By my calculations," I said, "that comes out to no school ever. I like it."

"Me too."

The substitute teacher said, "Hush, girls. You two, in the back! I don't want to have to speak to you again!"

It would have been entirely fine with me if she didn't speak to us again, but next thing I knew, she was calling my name.

"Will Marla Feinstein please raise her hand?" she said. So I did.

"Oh, it's you." As she walked toward me, she told the class, "Mrs. Guyer thought you might like to make Christmas—I mean, *holiday*—decorations. Won't that be fun?"

Teachers always give us dumb stuff to do before vacation and call it "fun." It's because they're so, so sick of us, they start to get desperate. Our regular teacher, Mrs. Guyer, was the one who was having fun—she'd taken the day off.

"Someone should tell the sub we're in fourth grade, not kindergarten," Lucy whispered. Her breath tickled my ear, making me giggle. But when the sub put a piece of blue paper and a piece of white paper on my desk, my giggles quit. I glanced down at the Hanukkah colors and watched the sub hand out red

and green paper to everyone else. My cheeks got hot.

Mrs. Guyer must have left a note for the sub saying there was one Jew in the class and I was it. A few days ago, before she abandoned us to this sub, Mrs. Guyer had me make a blue-and-white candle when the rest of the class made red-and-green ones. She talked about how everyone is different and that's what makes the world interesting. But everyone isn't different—just ME.

I wished myself out the window, on the playground, across the patchy lawn, on my Rollerblades, and zipping downhill, getting smaller in the distance—a tiny speck.

Then I heard Lucy's voice, loud and clear. "No fair!" she said. "I want the colors Marla got!"

The substitute's little lizard eyes flicked from side to side. "Oh!" she said. "Are you Jewish?"

"Totally," lied Lucy.

The sub squinted at Lucy's blond curls and turned-up Irish nose. Then she sighed and gave her blue and white paper too. Lucy made goofy faces behind the sub's back until I smiled.

I decided to make a white sailboat on a wide blue sea. But that was too hard, so I rolled my blue and white paper into a tube. I told Lucy that my brother could use it as a sword. Everything is a sword or a gun to him anyway.

Lucy, who is a great artist, cut her white paper into animal-shaped clouds and glued them to a blue sky. The whole blue-and-white business was way less icky since Lucy was working with Hanukkah colors too—but I was still glad to hear the bell ring.

My blue-and-white "decoration" was stuffed in my backpack. Lucy was waving hers around like a flag as we walked home from school. She sang, "Glory, glory hallelujah, teacher hit me with a ruler!" Then she poked me. "Hey, Marla, what's wrong with you?"

I wanted to sing. It was Friday. A weekend! And then only two more days of school until vacation! But I still felt a little creepy.

I pulled a lemon off of a neighbor's tree. "Catch!" I called—and Lucy did. We played catch while we walked, all the way to where I turn left and Lucy turns right.

My little brother, Ned, came charging out the front door, straight for me. He's always deliriously happy to see me after school. My mom says that's why I don't need a dog.

"Guess who came to school?" Ned said, grabbing at the ends of my long hair. "Guess!"

"Santa Claus," I said.

First Ned's face caved in, disappointed that I had guessed. Then he looked at me with awe, because I was so brilliant.

"I went to the same preschool, Neddy. Santa comes every year," I said.

"Oh." Ned thought about that, then perked up. "Guess what he gave me!"

I did not say, "A candy cane." That would have been mean.

"A CANDY CANE!" Ned said. He fished around in his grimy pocket with his grubby hand and pulled out a half-eaten, entirely slimed, candy cane. "Want some?" he offered.

A fabulous sister might have pretended to take a lick and made extravagant yum-yum sounds. Instead I reached into my backpack and pulled out my blue-and-white tube sword.

"Happy Hanukkah," I said. "Ho ho ho." No one

on earth would be excited by that crumpled scrap—except Ned. It must be nice to be three.

Ned jumped around, jabbing me with his wrinkled sword while I put on my Rollerblades. It occurred to me that he moved more like a tree frog than like any kind of mammal. I told him I'd be back before dinner, but still he watched me leave as if I was going off to war, on the moon.

Rollerblading is the best feeling in the world. It is like sliding on a really smooth wood floor in socks, except better, because you go and go and you're outside. My arms love it, my face loves it, even my hair loves it. And it's hilly in California where I live, with lots of glorious downhills to fly.

I'd had a great pre-dinner ride and was racing back home in the near-dark when Christmas lights started coming on at every house but ours. Lucy likes the pure white lights best, but I think the all-different-colored ones are perfect.

When I asked why we can't have Christmas lights, my mom said, "Because we're Jewish."

"What's that got to do with it?" I'd asked. "They

don't make you prove you're Christian at the store when you try to buy lights."

As I zipped toward home, I thought about the Christmas lights. They reminded me again about being singled out at school. Here it was the first night of Hanukkah, but you'd never know it was anything special looking at my house. As I got closer, I saw how boring and sad it looked—the plain, dull frump at a ball full of dazzling princesses. I knew exactly how it must feel.

C H A P T E R
•••••••••• 2 ••••••••••

This Hanukkah promised to be like all our other ones, only worse, because this time my dad wasn't going to be home.

My dad is a segment producer for a TV show, which means he makes pieces of the show, not the whole thing. They call his kind of show a "news magazine." There are three or four segments for each show: Maybe one on some extra-nasty crime or some wacky cult, then one about an amazingly brave person with an icky disease, or some evil threat to the environment, and last, a "warm-fuzzy-feel-good segment," as my dad calls them, "to calm everyone down enough to go to sleep."

Dad has been in the warm-fuzzy department a lot lately. The story he has been working on is about the sextuplets in Washington, D.C. That's six babies who were born at once, out of one human mother.

"That poor, poor woman," Mom had said, way back when my dad first started filming the sextuplets. Since then Dad has flown to Washington to produce one sextuplet segment after another, and we are all sick to death of them.

In the beginning he'd said the sextuplets looked like a bunch of pink raisins, and they sort of gave him the willies. Now he says they have "individual person-alities" and HE can tell them all apart.

"The network feels that if I stick Santa hats on all six heads, it will be a holiday hit," my dad had said yes-terday. "So I'm taking the red-eye back to Washington tonight."

"Cookie has red eyes," Ned said. That's the pet white rat at his preschool.

"I wouldn't be a bit surprised if Cookie had the seat next to me!" Dad said. "I often sit next to rats who snore. Or worse, rats who wake me up to tell me *I* snore." My dad thinks he's hilarious.

"Daddy's just kidding," Mom said, shooting Dad one of her looks.

So my dad told Ned that it's called a red-eye flight because you get so tired being on an airplane all night that you get red eyes.

"You'll see," he said, "when I get home."

When we got up this morning, my dad was gone.

Anyway, it was the first night of Hanukkah, so my mom got out the menorah (that's the Hanukkah candle holder). I lit the shammes (that's the candle that you light all the other candles with). Then I handed the shammes to Ned, who nearly roasted himself and dripped wax everywhere while somehow managing to get his candle lit.

My mom and I sang the song we always sing when we light the candles, and Ned barked along.

Oh Hanukkah, oh Hanukkah, come light the menorah!
Let's have a party, we'll all dance the hora.
Gather 'round the table, we'll give you a treat.
A dreidel to play with, and latkes to eat.

And while we are playing, the candles are burning low.
One for each night, they shed a sweet light,
To remind us of days long ago.
One for each night, they shed a sweet light,
To remind us of days long ago.

"We don't dance the hora," I said. "Why does the song say we dance the hora?"

"Because it rhymes with 'MENORAH'!" my mom said. "Should it say we'll go to the store-ah? Sit on the floor-ah? Invite cousin Laura? What if some Jew somewhere doesn't have a cousin Laura?"

I knew that the fastest way to get through the whole stupid thing was to not ask any more questions, but one slipped out. "So which 'days long ago' are we supposed to be reminded of anyway?"

"It's that war between King Whatshisname and the Maccabees," my mom said, shoving her slippery brown hair behind her ears, like she does.

Ned and I didn't know what she was talking about, so she told us the Hanukkah story. Mom's version:

"Two thousand years ago the Jews were minding their own business, going to Temple to worship their one God. Everyone else at the time was into multiple gods and idols and whatnot.

"Anyway, the bad guy, King . . . Antiochus, came along and said, 'From now on it is against the law to be Jewish, and anyone who observes any Jewish tradition will be punished as a criminal, taken as a slave, beaten up, and killed. And if you don't put Christmas lights on your Temple, then I am going to huff and puff and blow it down!' "

"MOM!" I said. "There were no Christmas lights two thousand years ago. They didn't even have electricity!"

"Well, if you want to get picky about it," my mom said, "there were no Christians or Christmas yet either. But that's not the point.

"A Jewish family called the Maccabees," my mom went on, "said, 'Not by the hair of our chinny-chin-chins!' So the king's soldiers blew the Temple down. Then they did the rest of the usual rotten war stuff."

Ned started making machine-guns sounds.

"Guns hadn't been invented yet, sorry," my mom told him. "Maybe swords or slingshots or something."

Ned's gun noises made me think of my dad. If he were here, he would probably put in antiaircraft missiles and sound effects like explosions and dying groans. That's what he does with the Civil War.

Ned thinks that stuff is a hoot. I think both my parents are bizarre.

My mom pushed her hair back and said, "The

Maccabees fought using sticks and stones and stuff. They were just a tiny band of Jews against the king's powerful army. Miracle number one: The Jews won.

"Then they fixed up the Temple. They wanted to relight their lamp to celebrate, but the bad guys had spilled the sacred oil with all their huffing and puffing. There was only enough oil left to last one measly night.

"Miracle number two—like when my gas gauge is on empty and yet we make it to the gas station: The oil burned for eight nights instead of just one. The end."

I suspected that Jewish people the world over were listening to this story told differently. Less huffing and puffing, for one thing. My fault, I was the one who had asked her.

My mom handed Ned and me each a bag from the grocery store and said, "Sorry, I didn't get a chance to wrap them."

In Ned's bag was a pair of socks that he immediately put on his hands and used as boxing gloves— happy as a clam.

In my bag were six rolls of Scotch tape. When I did not act happy as another clam, my mom explained, "So you'll stop using mine all the time."

"Gee, you shouldn't have," I said to make her feel guilty, but it didn't work.

My mom just shrugged and said, "You're welcome."

My overnight bag was packed. I was going to sleep over at Lucy's. She and I had something special planned, something secret, and this Hanukkah business had already taken up a lot of time.

"We're supposed to let the candles melt," my mom said, "but you can't walk to Lucy's in the dark and I can't leave them burning while I drive you." She was about to blow them out when I stopped her.

I don't know why I didn't want her to do that—I just didn't. "If we can't have Christmas because we are so Jewish," I said, "then let's at least be Jewish!"

"We are Jewish no matter what, Marla," my mom said, but we waited. It didn't take long for the candles to melt and they looked kind of nice, though not compared to how Lucy's house looked when we pulled in her driveway. Her dad had hung lights *everywhere*.

I love going to Lucy's house. It is totally different than mine. All the furniture is dark and there are no baby toys around. Her two big sisters have makeup and other teenage stuff in the bathroom. Their dad doesn't have much in the way of knickknacks, but their mom collects everything—teacups, thimbles, little cat statues displayed in glass cases like a museum. Lucy's grandma lives there too and has old clocks that make noise. Three or four of them chimed just as I walked in.

"Hi!" Lucy said, then whispered, "Ready for the you-know-what?"

"The moon is full," I whispered in return.

We needed a private spot for our séance. A spot where no one would know that we had matches.

We took that blue-and-white candle I'd made at school, and some matches from Lucy's dad's desk, up to Lucy's room, but Kate was there, in one of her porcupine moods. It's supposed to be half Lucy's room, but it isn't really, at least not when Kate is like that. We tried her oldest sister Yaz's room, but we couldn't go in there either because she was on the phone with the door closed. And we aren't allowed in Lucy's parents' room or her grandma's— ever.

Downstairs Lucy's father was reading the paper in the living room and her grandma was watching TV in the den.

"I'll bet you a million bucks your mom's in the kitchen," I said. "Why is she always in there anyway? My mom's never in the kitchen."

"I think she's under a spell," Lucy said, "doing dishes for eternity."

We looked in the kitchen, and sure enough, there was Mrs. Doyle with her dish towel, humming along with the Christmas carols on the radio. Lucy and I both started laughing.

"What's so funny?" Lucy's mom smiled, ready to laugh with us.

So we bolted from the kitchen into the tiny bathroom next to the pantry. I was laughing so hard, I had to pee.

We locked the bathroom door, and lit the blue-and-white candle. It's a good thing that Lucy had insisted on keeping that candle when I wanted to throw it out, because it was just right for a séance.

We turned off the light. In the dark with the candle between us on the floor, I instantly started feeling

spooked. My arm hairs tingled. My toes curled in my sandals.

"What should we ask?" I whispered.

We could hear "Rudolph the Red-Nosed Reindeer" playing on Lucy's mom's radio.

"Let's call the spirit of the guy who wrote that song," Lucy said. "I want to know if Rudolph forgave Prancer and Dancer and those other bullies for being so mean to him."

Lucy put on a scary low voice and said, "Whoever you are, dead songwriter... I wish we knew his name..."

"Cut it out!" I said. "You're blowing out the candle!"

"I am not! You are!" Lucy said, and we both started screaming. The candle went out and we couldn't find the light switch, so we screamed louder. Someone started pounding on the bathroom door, and they were yelling pretty loud too.

When we finally found the light and the doorknob and came out of the bathroom, Lucy's entire family was lined up in the hallway, a whole row of curly blond heads. Everyone in the row had angry blue eyes except Yaz, who was smiling. I want to be Yaz when I am a teenager.

Lucy's father said he was sending me straight home for playing with matches.

But he didn't.

We promised to be very quiet the rest of the night.

But we weren't.

In bed later I asked Lucy what she would do if she was Rudolph and everyone was picking on her for having a shiny nose.

"I know," she said. "When Santa asked me to guide his sleigh, I'd tell him to fire all the other reindeer and hire elephants or something."

"And make Prancer and Dancer take turns sweeping up after them, like the guy at the circus!" I said.

Kate told us we were silly, infantile, obnoxious, and a few other things. Then she took her blanket and pillow into Yaz's room.

But actually my question was kind of serious. Poor old Rudolph ... it wasn't easy being different.

CHAPTER

·········· 3 ··········

By the time Lucy and I dragged ourselves out of bed, everyone else was awake. Mrs. Doyle was in the kitchen, of course, and Lucy's grandma and sisters were putting up Christmas decorations in the living room.

Mrs. Doyle's ornament collection is famous around here. She has zillions. Lucy and I decided to help decorate.

"You can start on those," said Yaz.

Inside the big boxes that Yaz had pointed to were littler boxes. As Lucy and I unwrapped each ornament, it was like opening a tiny present. They were all different. All so pretty.

Lucy's grandmother, who thinks we are still babies, said, "Remember, girls, Santa does not bring toys to little girls who break ornaments!"

"Santa's taste must be as corny as my mom's," whispered Lucy. "Look at that tacky elf."

"It's not tacky," I said, setting it in a cloud of cotton on the mantel. "It's cute."

"Does your mom collect?" Yaz asked me. "Hanukkah stuff, I mean?"

I tried to imagine my mom collecting *anything.* It was an impossible picture. And what would anyone collect for Hanukkah? "Hanukkah's not like that," I said. "It's … It's …"

The sisters and even Grandma looked at me to explain.

"It's at the same time as Christmas, but it's just nothing like it," I said.

"What *is* it like?" Kate asked.

"Well," I said, "Bubbi, that's my grandma, sends us candles from Michigan. Then we light the menorah and sing a Hanukkah song. Then my parents give me a gift. It's always something useful, though, never anything great, and almost never wrapped. Then, around the fourth night, we forget to light the candles and by the time anyone remembers, Hanukkah is over. So my brother and I get whatever gifts are left and that's that." I shrugged. "Hanukkah."

Grandma and the sisters looked at each other. I guess I'd made Hanukkah sound pretty dull.

Suddenly, SMASH! A huge red ornament lay shattered in countless shiny bits on the floor. Lucy's mom came running out of the kitchen with her dish towel.

"Sorry, Mom," Lucy giggled. "I slipped. Guess there's no Santa for Marla OR me this year. Right, Grandma?"

We all looked over at Lucy's grandmother. She was scowling like an old toad. But at least everyone had stopped expecting me to recite " 'Twas the Night Before Hanukkah" or something.

After breakfast at Lucy's I stumbled home. I must have fallen asleep on the back-porch swing because the next thing I knew, Ned was sticking a leaf up my nose and I was buried under a heap of his stuffed animals.

"Look at you," my mom said when I dragged myself into the house. "This is precisely why I hate sleepovers."

I hung out in my room most of the day, coming out only to call Lucy now and then. Kate kept answering the phone and she called me a pest.

When my stomach said it was dinnertime, I went out to our white kitchen. No mom. Our white living room? Nope. Dining room? Bedrooms? One empty, white room after another. I once heard my mom tell a friend that her first choice would be to decorate strictly with invisible furniture but since that was not an option, white was the next best thing. "Anything else would require making a decision, and I'm tired of making decisions," she'd said.

Finally I banged on my mom's office door. There she was, working at her computer. She is a personal bookkeeper for two rich old men and their rich young wives. My mom pays their bills. She also tells us how much money they spend. This year one couple had a two-thousand-dollar Christmas tree, like the ones in department stores, put up in their house. They didn't personally hang one single strand of tinsel.

Anyway, there she was at her desk. Ned was on the floor drawing with markers—on his face mostly, and his clothes and arms and the floor, with just a tiny scribble on his piece of paper.

"I'm hungry," I said.

"Oh." My mom blinked through her bug-eyed reading glasses. "What time is it?"

"Time to eat," I said.

"Well, be a sweetie, Marla, and go to my recipe drawer, please," my mom said.

Her "recipe drawer" as she calls it, has never had a recipe in it in its life. That's where she shoves all the carryout, fast-food menus that collect on our porch.

My mom calls herself "cooking-impaired" and tells people she's no good at "kitchen sports." They think it's funny. I don't.

I dug out a flyer for pizza, and ordered a large, with pineapple. I figured that if I had to do all the work, then I could choose the toppings.

Mom came out to pay the delivery guy and we ate while the pizza was hot.

Then my dad called from Washington. Ned talked first, as always. When it was my turn, my dad told me he was sticking the six Santa hats on the six baby heads. "Then I just have to make it as heartwarming as possible in editing, and come home." My mom

25
◆

always talks to my dad last, lovey-dovey stuff. She whispers and giggles. I think it's gross when old people act like that.

After my mom hung up, she got the menorah and lit the shammes. Ned and I each lit one candle for the second night of Hanukkah and we sang the song again.

When we got to the "a dreidel to play with" part, I looked at the hollow, green, plastic one that Bubbi had sent to us. The gold foil candy coins that came inside it were long gone. We had gobbled them up the second the dreidel had come in the mail.

"It doesn't spin," I said.

"Well, they are supposed to be made of clay," my mom said, "or wood or something."

When I asked her how to play, she said, "It's gambling, for chocolate gelt. 'Gelt' is money. One of these Hebrew letters on it is a gimel, as in 'gimmie a gimel and some gelt.'"

"You don't have a clue how to play, do you?" I asked her.

"Not a clue," she agreed. "But we can make up a game."

I did *not* want to make up a game. Here we were

not able to have Christmas lights because being Jewish was so very important and we didn't do the hora and my mom didn't even know which letter was the GIMEL!

I went to my room. A long time later my mom knocked and came in. She left my present at the foot of my bed, kissed the top of my head, and said, "Happy Hanukkah."

She forgot to close my door behind her.

CHAPTER

• • • • • • • • • 4 • • • • • • • •

After breakfast the next morning I took a shower. My hair is so thick that it takes forever to dry and the back of my shirt gets soaked. I was twirling in the front yard letting the sun dry it, getting dizzy, and thinking I should just cut my hair short like Lucy's, when she came zipping around the corner on her bike, Lemonade.

Lucy's sister Kate had named it Lemonade when it was new and bright-yellow. It wasn't bright-yellow anymore. Ever since it was handed down to Lucy, she has tried to change its name, but none of the new names stick.

Lucy parked Lemonade next to Misty. Misty is my pale blue-gray bike, the color of fog. Misty and Lemonade are, needless to say, best friends.

As soon as Lucy pulled off her helmet, the expression on her face made me panic.

"What's wrong?" I asked.

"MAAAARLA!" Lucy wailed, "I have to go to Texas! Tomorrow! For five whole days!"

"WHAT?" I shrieked. "WHY?"

"Some great-aunt I've never even met is really sick. She is Grandma's eighty-one-year-old baby sister, and Grandma's afraid to travel all the way to Texas alone—and she really wants to see her before she dies—I'm sure Grandma's sister is a very nice old lady and I'm sorry she's so sick and all—but—"

I could hardly hear what Lucy was saying. My mind kept picturing the endless days without her.

"So my mom is going to take Grandma to Texas to see this sick aunt, and my dad thinks me and my sisters will love Texas, and so—" Lucy's face scrunched up and I could tell she was about to cry.

"But we have so much planned!" I said. Actually we had nothing at all planned, and we'd really been looking forward to our nothing.

Then I got an idea. "I know!" I said. "What if you stayed at my house?"

Lucy lit up for the first time. Then she dimmed down. "Nah, it's Christmas. My parents will want us all together."

"But last year Kate went skiing over the holiday recess," I said. "And didn't Yaz leave town too one year?"

We agreed that it was worth a try, and so we went to find my mom in her office.

"FOUR sleep-overs in a row?" my mom gasped.

Lucy and I begged.

My mom made us promise we'd clean up my entire room, including the stuff under my bed. We swore we would be nice to Ned and quiet at night. We'd cheerfully do laundry, dishes, and vacuuming. We'd be helpful, helpful, helpful and never complain about anything. That was when she said, "Fine."

We knew she'd be easy. The tricky one was going to be Lucy's mother.

We tried to coach my mom about what to say. "They'll save oodles of money on not buying me a plane ticket," Lucy said.

"And the hotel," I added, "one less bed."

"Plus I'd miss school!" Lucy said. "I can't miss school!"

"That's right!" I said, "There's still Monday and Tuesday! And we always do really, really important stuff right before vacation!" I rolled my eyes at Lucy, but she kept a perfectly straight face.

My mom insisted she could handle it herself and made us leave the room while she called Lucy's mother.

We huddled outside my mom's office door. Lucy's fingers dug into my arm. My fingers were probably digging into hers.

From the little bits we heard, it sounded like, "poor woman is so sick, so old ... hospital ... Lucy is so sensitive, so young ... upsetting ..." And we figured out that my mom meant that Lucy might freak out or be in the way at the hospital, or if the great-aunt died and there was a funeral and stuff. The mothers talked and talked and talked it over.

It didn't look entirely hopeless, so Lucy got back on Lemonade and went home to work on her mom from that end. This was a tricky move because if we lost and Lucy had to leave the next day, then we were wasting our last day together being apart. If it worked, though, it would be worth this one day to have five unbroken days in a row.

The phone frenzy went on and on with one mom calling the other back, three-and-a-half seconds after they'd hung up. I knew Lucy was going just as buggy as me, at her house.

Mrs. Doyle changed her mind seven or eight times, but at least every now and then it sounded like a YES. During the YES moments between calls, MY mom would threaten to change HER mind too! She said that if I didn't do this and this and that, she was going to call Lucy's mother "THIS INSTANT" and cancel the whole thing once and for all.

I sat in our blindingly white kitchen, waiting for the white phone to ring with a Lucy-sleep-over-update. I knew it would help our case if I rinsed the white breakfast dishes that were piled in the white sink, but I just sat at the white kitchen table fiddling with that stupid green plastic dreidel, trying to make it spin. I thought it might work if it wasn't so light and hollow, so I filled it with Cheerios, but that didn't help.

Lucy called and said her mom was taking her out to run errands, and she'd call me later. It had already been the longest day in the history of the world, and it wasn't even lunchtime!

The suspense was making me crazy and I had to get out of the house, so I shoved the plastic dreidel into my pocket, grabbed my Rollerblades, and whizzed up to Joe's Deli.

I have tons of Jewish relatives back in Michigan, where Mom comes from, but Joe and Joe's wife at the deli were the only Jewish people I could think of here in California.

"LOOK WHO'S HERE!" Joe yelled as soon as I rolled in. "IT'S OUR LITTLE MARLA!"

Joe's wife, whose name, as far as I knew, was "Joe's Wife," poked her head up from under the counter. "LITTLE MARLA!" she hollered.

My dad once told me that Joe and his wife reminded him of a radio he used to have. The control knob was stuck on top volume so it could only BLAST!

My mom calls Joe and Joe's Wife "THE LOUD CROWD." But I like them. I don't even mind that they always call me "LITTLE."

Joe and Joe's Wife asked me about school and Lucy and my mom and brother and dad, and the sextuplets. They are big fans of the sextuplets. They've watched every segment in my dad's series.

I wanted to say, "STOP WATCHING!" because as long as people watch one stupid Raisin segment after another, the network will keep sending my dad to Washington. But I didn't.

When Joe and Joe's Wife were done asking me about everyone, and after they'd offered me tastes of salami and free cookies, they asked me what they could do for me, "A NICE RYE?"

"I'm here for information," I said. "Hanukkah information."

They both crowded closer and peered over the counter.

"It's dreidels," I said.

"OH! DREIDELS," yelled Joe's Wife, clapping her hands like a door slamming. "WE HAVE DREIDELS!" She rummaged around behind the cash register and brought out three wooden dreidels, which she pushed toward me.

"But how do you play?" I asked. "What are the letters? One is a gimel, right?"

So Joe and Joe's Wife gave me a dreidel lesson. I was talking loudly myself by the time I left. Yelling is contagious.

Back home Mom said Lucy had called to say YES! I twitched every time the phone rang, afraid that Lucy's mom would change her mind again. If we could just get through this night, we'd be safe.

Meanwhile, it was the third night of Hanukkah. After the candles and the song and dinner, I pulled out my wooden dreidel with a "Taa-daa! Look what Joe's Wife at the deli gave me!

"This is a nun," I said, pointing. "This is a shin, here's a heh, and this one, Mom, is the gimel! And I know why dreidels go with Hanukkah."

"WHY DO DREIDELS GO WITH HANUK-KAH?" yelled my mom in her LOUD CROWD imitation.

"Guess!" I said.

"War. Demolished Temple. Oil ... spinning tops? I give up," my mom said, tucking back a clump of hair.

"Remember that evil creep, King Whatshis-name?" I asked.

"Antiochus," said my mom.

"Well, he ordered his soldiers to barge into houses without knocking, to make sure nobody was doing anything Jewish, like praying or reading holy books or anything. So the Jews kept these tops around as de-coys. Whenever the soldiers came in, the Jews would hide their religious stuff and pretend they were just sit-ting around gambling. Neat, huh?"

Joe and Joe's Wife had said we could play for walnuts, but we used the pennies out of my mom's junk drawer. We divided them up so we each had eight, like the eight nights of Hanukkah.

"Now everyone puts one penny into the center of the table," I explained.

"No! They're MINE!" Ned shrieked, clutching his pennies.

My mom worked on him for a while and finally he agreed to part with the one that was the least shiny.

"You spin the dreidel," I said, "and if it lands on the nun, you do nothing. If it lands on gimel, you take the whole pot. If it lands on heh, you take half the pot, and if it falls on the shin, you put one penny in."

"And you do not put pennies in your mouth," my mom told Ned.

"And," I continued, "the four letters stand for 'A Great Miracle Happened There.' Nes Gadol Hayah Sham."

"How did you remember all that?" Mom asked.

I had to remind her and Ned which letter was which for the whole game.

When my dad called that night, I told him we were playing dreidels. "A great miracle happened there,"

Dad said, "and I don't mean the Maccabees! I mean you and Ned and Mommy playing dreidels!" And he laughed.

I didn't forget the Hebrew letters, but I almost forgot about Lucy while my mom and my brother and I spun dreidels. We played until NED, of all people, won everyone's pile of pennies.

When my mom came in my room to say good night, she sat on the edge of my bed. "What an interesting little girl you are," she said, petting my hair like I was a cat.

Now if Lucy really comes here tomorrow, I thought, instead of going to stupid Texas, everything will be perfect.

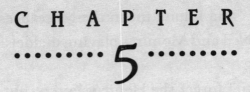
Early, early before school Monday morning I looked out the window and saw Lucy's dad's car pull up in front of my house. I ran outside, holding my breath, until Lucy tossed her suitcase out onto the lawn. HOORAY!

There was that last tense moment when my mom leaned into their car window and talked way too long to Lucy's parents. But finally the car pulled away from the curb. Lucy and I jumped around yelling, "YA-HOOO!"

Then off we went to school, like twin sisters who live in the same house. We planned to switch seats and switch names and everything if there was another sub, but Mrs. Guyer was back.

After school we built a ship out of lawn furniture and sheets and we were playing that we were orphan stowaways crossing the sea to America, but Ned kept poking his head in, spitting and making gross noises.

"Mom!" I yelled. "Ned's bugging us!"

She came to her office door and said, "Is that a complaint I hear? What has it been, twenty minutes since you've been home, and I'm already hearing a *complaint*?"

I wanted to Rollerblade to Main Street, but Lucy really didn't want to. Rollerblading is the absolute only thing Lucy and I don't have in common. I wish, wish, wish she could love that feeling of flying like I do. I think she should just practice more, but she says it's her ankles. Anyway, we took our bikes, Lemonade and Misty.

At our favorite restaurant, The Toasted Bun, we got such a hopeless attack of giggles watching two teenagers kissing that Lucy got soda up her nose.

Then we went in and out of the shops.

"Your mom has more Christmas decorations than all these stores put together," I said. "Look. This angel looks exactly like you!" I showed her a sweet little figurine with blond curls.

Lucy rolled her eyes. "It looks like one of the Raisins to me," she said, and she was right. How come

I never noticed before that my dad's sextuplets look like baby Lucys?

"I just don't get the snowflakes and snowmen everywhere," Lucy said. "It's eighty degrees today!"

"Santa must get awfully sweaty when he hits California," I agreed.

Lucy wound up a music box and it plinked out "Jingle Bells." "See? 'Dashing through the *snow*.'" Then she asked me if Hanukkah has weather.

"I don't know. I don't think so," I said.

"We'll ask your mom," Lucy said.

"My mom," I said, "won't know."

Every time a salesperson said, "Merry Christmas" to us, Lucy said, "Happy Hanukkah."

Lucy asked the card store lady if she had any Hanukkah decorations. "No? Any music boxes that play Hanukkah tunes? How about Hanukkah wrapping paper?"

"Cut it out," I told her.

"Cut what out?"

"All this Hanukkah stuff," I said. "You're embarrassing everyone."

"Everyone who? The saleslady?" Lucy laughed.

I didn't want to say "everyone me," so I laughed too.

I was getting a little afraid that Lucy had traded away her Christmas with her family thinking Hanukkah was going to be an equal hoot.

When Lucy and I came into the kitchen that evening we found my mom grating up potatoes while talking long-distance to Bubbi. "No," she said, "I do not have a *Cuisinart*, I've got this razor-sharp metal thing with holes. Isn't my blood and the flesh from my knuckles supposed to give latkes that special flavor?"

"Gross, Mom!" I said.

When she hung up the phone, she turned to Lucy and me and announced, "Hanukkah Performance Art." Then she began dropping globs of the ground-up potato goo into the sizzling frying pan.

She burnt herself on spattering oil about fifty times. With each burn she winced and reminded us that she had never done this before.

"I hope you appreciate this, Marla," she said, "because you are my inspiration."

And I hadn't even asked for latkes! Yet.

"This is Hanukkah food, right?" Lucy asked.

"It says so in the song," my mom said.

"What song?" asked Lucy. "Does it have snow?"

Mom looked confused. "Snow?"

I stood by my mom at the stove and she and I sang "Oh Hanukkah" for Lucy. Ned shrieked along with us, leaping around the kitchen like a tree frog. I thought about my dad's deep singing voice, but I didn't mention it.

"Hey! I bet it's because latkes are cooked in oil!" I said, suddenly getting it.

"What is?"

"You know, like the *Miracle of Oil*? So we eat oily stuff on Hanukkah?" I said.

"Sounds good to me," said my mom.

When we finally sat down to eat, Mom said, "The real miracle of oil is how fabulous it makes a potato taste, cardiovascular disaster or no." And she was right. They were great.

"What was Hanukkah like when you were a kid?" Lucy asked my mom.

"Well, we hitched our old plow horse, Ruby, up to the cart, bundled ourselves up in blankets, and headed off through the snows of Michigan to Auntie Eva's cabin in the woods...." Mom said.

Ned asked, "You had a horse?"

"Don't talk with your mouth full," my mom said.

"Come on, Mom," I said, "tell us for real."

"Hanukkah when I was a kid ..." she said.

Lucy and I looked at each other while my mom sat staring at her fork. Then Mom said, "It was a madhouse. There were so many of us, Uncle Larry and me, and Bubbi and Poppa..."

"That's my mom's brother," I told Lucy, "and my grandparents."

"And there were all the aunts ... Marla, do you remember Auntie Eva? Actually she would have been your great-aunt. Oh. You were too young. In fact, you weren't born...."

My mom stared at nothing some more and Ned got fidgety.

"Mom!" I said after a while. "Are you going to tell us or not?"

My mom looked at me and Lucy and Ned as if she didn't know who we were, and then she laughed.

"Right. Hanukkah when I was little. It was wild. There were, let me see, Auntie Eva had four kids,

Selma had three... Rusty and Bernice each had two. How many cousins is that? And a bunch of uncles, and..."

"You all had horses?" Ned asked.

"No, baby," my mom said, "Fords and Chevys. It was Detroit, after all."

I was afraid Mom would fade out again so I said, "And..."

"And..." my mom continued, "we'd all cram into Auntie Eva's apartment. A two-bedroom walk-up. And there was always the big debate about whose latkes were better. I liked them thin and crisp, but my cousin Andrea liked the fat, fall-apart kind.

"All the aunts brought their latkes on trays to heat up in the oven, except for Auntie Eva, who was frying them fresh in her teeny kitchen, with all four burners going.

"Cousins Robert and Alan would chase each other around, slugging it out, knocking over lamps. And Auntie Eva's mean little yippy dog would be frantic.... The uncles would smoke cigars. Cousins Laurie and Susie would poke through the grab-bag gifts calling dibs.... Babies were put down to sleep on the pile of coats on the bed...and their mothers would try to hush us...."

My mom's voice drifted away again. She sat hooking a hank of her hair behind her ear, only for it to unhook immediately and need hooking again. I bet she doesn't even know she does that a million times a day.

By this time Ned had wandered off to play with his trucks. Lucy and I got up and started clearing the table and loading the dishwasher.

"My mom never finishes her stories about back then," I told Lucy. "She either starts crying, remembering dead people, or she just zones out into space like that."

When Dad called, I let Ned shriek into the phone awhile. Then I grabbed it away from him and said, "Dad, you won't believe this, but Mom made latkes tonight!"

There was a big noise. Then my dad said, "That sound was me falling off my chair!"

"We saved you some of the latke stuff. You can have it when you get home tomorrow," I told him.

"I'm sorry, sweetpea," he said. "I'd give anything to see Mommy making latkes, but it doesn't look like I'm going to make it tomorrow. Marla? Marla, are you there?"

I gave the phone to my mom.

CHAPTER
·········· 6 ··········

The last day of school! And only a half a day! Lucy and I agreed that no matter what dumb "fun" Mrs. Guyer came up with, we could get through a half a day. And we did.

When we got home, Ned was acting weird, the way he does when my dad has been gone too long. I mean, he acts plenty weird always, but he gets even worse. He was half weepy and clingy, and half mean and violent. A truly annoying combination.

My mom told us that Ned was driving her nuts and she had a ton of work to do, so Lucy said we'd be *glad* to take him out for a while.

"I can't believe you said that!" I hissed.

"We promised your mom that we'd help..." Lucy said.

When I made a face at her, she said, "It'll be fun!"

"Fun?" I scowled at Lucy, thinking, Sure, as "fun"

as making blue-and-white decorations. Baby-sitting Ned was precisely how I did not want to begin my vacation.

My mom raised her eyebrows and looked from me to Lucy and back again. I feared a helpful lecture, so I said, "Fine. We'll take him, but Lucy is watching him. Not me!"

"It will be my pleasure," Lucy told my mom in her goody-goody voice.

About the only place close enough to walk with Ned is the library two blocks away. I did not want to go to the library. But Lucy said she did, and Ned was wildly excited.

They acted stupid on the way there. They thought they were so funny, walking like elephants, then apes, and making animal noises. What if someone saw us? I started walking faster and Lucy told me that I was being an old poop. Ned thought that was hilarious.

I walked even faster and got to the library first. I was inside, looking at some books, when I saw them SWIM through the door like fish.

I couldn't believe I'd thought of that girl as my best friend! It made me totally ill to think I'd be stuck with her twenty-four hours a day for three more days.

I hid from them behind the stacks. Then I sneaked up to Ms. Mindy's desk.

"Do you have any books on Hanukkah?" I asked in a whisper.

"Oh, yes," she whispered back.

She led me around to a shelf. "Well, here's one, sort of," she said. "At least there must be something about Hanukkah in here. . . ." It was a short book on Jewish holidays. "Teachers check them out this time of year," Ms. Mindy apologized.

"Well, how about music?" I asked. "Jewish music, like for horas?"

Ms. Mindy brightened up. "We do have that!"

I checked out the cassette and the book and slipped out of the library without Lucy or Ned spotting me.

I was in my room, listening to the tape on my Walkman and trying to guess how to do the hora, when my mom came in.

"Where's Ned?" she asked, instantly worried about her precious baby.

"Who knows and who cares," I said.

"I do, so tell," she said. "Now."

"He's at the library. With Lucy," I said. "All right?"

"Not all right," she said. "You march right back to that library this instant, Miss Marla, and get your brother—"

But just then we heard the front door open and Ned and Lucy came in. My mom shot me a look, then turned and walked out of my room. She forgot to close the door behind her, so I did—SLAM.

Even I know the hora is a circle dance and not something you do alone, so I turned off the music and read a little. I wrote in my diary about Lucy being such a traitor. I polished my nails, and looked in the mirror for pimples. Then I was bored. Then I was really bored. Then really, really bored.

I heard my mom tell Ned to get in the car to go to the market with her.

He said, "No."

She said, "Yes."

He said, "No."

She said, "I'll buy you a cookie."

I heard the car pull out of the driveway, and then I heard nothing at all.

There was a lot of silence. I wondered if Lucy had gone to the store too. I opened my door a sliver to hear better and there was Lucy, fist raised, about to knock. We both jumped back, surprised. I don't know which of us laughed first. Me or my best friend.

When we went into the kitchen at dinnertime, my mom said she'd been cleaning the grease from the stove for hours, so we could forget a latke encore. "Anyway, the leftover potato stuff turned creepy-looking in the fridge," she said.

We made tuna sandwiches, lit the candles, and sang our song. Then I told everyone I had a surprise.

"Menorah music!" Ned said.

"Hora music," Lucy corrected him. "Ms. Mindy told us."

"She tattled?" I asked. "Ms. Mindy?"

"Well, I guess I went up to her right after you did," Lucy said, "and we both asked for books on Hanukkah, and she knows we're best friends...."

I decided not to be mad.

"Hora music, eh?" my mom muttered, shaking her head.

We all looked at her. She shrugged and said, "If we must, we must."

As we trooped into the living room, my mom

said, "I'm going to have to dig pretty deep to remember this. I probably haven't danced the hora since Uncle Larry's wedding, so bear with me."

We put on the tape and took hands, and it seemed like my mom remembered instantly. Her feet turned this way then that and gave a little jump and a kick. And she dragged us stumbling around and around in our circle of giggles.

When the phone rang, we had to stop. But I said, "We can't talk, Dad. Mom is teaching us to hora."

"Did you say HORA?" my dad said. "I must have the wrong number. I'll call back later."

Ned's feet got tangled easily, but even he more or less got the general idea. We all jumped and kicked and whirled in a circle and landed in a happy, sweaty heap at the end.

"Voilà. Hora!" my mom panted.

"Sorry about today," I said when Lucy and I were in our beds that night.

"Me too," Lucy said. "I always wanted a little brother or sister."

"You've got two sisters!" I said.

"Yeah, but I'm the baby. No one looks up to me

like Ned looks up to you. He's thrilled if you just sneeze in his direction."

"I've always wanted your big sisters," I said. "They treat you like a doll."

"Exactly," Lucy said. "Which sounds better? To be a doll that's played with awhile, then left half-dressed with your head facing backward in the dust and dirty socks under the bed—or to be worshipped like a queen?"

"You win." I giggled. "Maybe Ned isn't so bad after all."

CHAPTER
·········· 7 ··········

The next day Lucy was brushing my hair on the back-porch swing when she said, "Tonight is Christmas Eve."

"I know," I said. "You're supposed to be eggnogging and singing carols and stuff, right?"

"Hmmm," Lucy said. "Something like that, but…"

While I was waiting for her to finish her sentence, I remembered her family's Christmas Eve party last year and my heart started thumping. There had been holly and pretty pine wreaths and stockings on the fireplace. Every inch of Lucy's house was decorated, even the bathrooms. The tree was gorgeous, lit up and loaded with tinsel and ornaments.

I remember how I'd felt crazy with jealousy that Lucy had all that and I didn't. I suddenly just had to have something for myself. When no one was looking, I slipped a teeny gingerbread house off the tree and put it in my pocket.

I'd wanted to have it in my pocket so badly, but as soon as it was there, I desperately wanted it out. I was scared that someone would catch me putting it back on the tree, though, so I just stood there—feeling miserable.

Then Lucy's sister Yaz came up and gave me a present! It was wrapped in candy cane paper with a silver bow. The tiny card had my name on it, and it wasn't from the whole family, meaning their mom, but just from Yaz. It was the absolute worst moment of my entire life.

Knowing the gingerbread house was in my pocket while Yaz, the coolest person I'd ever met, was being so sweet to me, had made me dizzy.

"Go on, open it," Yaz said.

So I did. I stared at it awhile, so busy feeling bad about the gingerbread house that my eyes could barely focus.

"It's a barrette," Yaz said. "A hair thing."

I guess I still looked dumb so she said, "Extra big to hold all your gorgeous thick hair."

Maybe I said, "Thanks," maybe not. I'm not sure.

After Yaz shrugged and walked away, I went into

the kitchen. It was mobbed with women laughing and bumping into each other and fixing more and more plates of food. I slipped into the pantry, where the trash basket was, and shoved the gingerbread house deep under the paper plates and other garbage. I've wondered a million times since then why I didn't leave it on a pantry shelf or something.

Just remembering that awful, awful night, even a whole year later, made me sick all over again.

Sitting on the swing I felt my neck prickle and I knew I had better hurry and change the subject. I glanced at Lucy, who was staring off in space thinking I-don't-know-what, maybe about the same Christmas party. I hadn't even noticed that she had stopped brushing my hair.

I didn't want her to ask me why I'd stopped swinging or why my face was beet-red, which it had to be.

I jumped up and said, "Race you to the fence? On your mark! Get set! Go!" And Lucy was on her feet—and racing past me.

"What can we do that's Christmasy?" I asked as we stood panting after our race.

"I was just wondering the exact same thing," she said. "Should we break into my house like robbers and have a look around at all the stuff?"

"That sounds creepy." I was picturing everything dark and empty, with all that dark furniture and Grandma's weird clocks going off. "My mom won't let us have a tree or anything *inside*..." I said. "But outdoors... no one could stop us from decorating outside, could they?"

We rushed to my room and rummaged around through drawers and shelves and boxes. We crammed everything into my backpack and a plastic grocery bag. Then we hopped on Lemonade and Misty and took off for the park.

We sneaked around, looking very carefully at tree after tree. It had to be hidden away and it had to be a pine and it had to be short enough that we could reach a lot of branches—and there it was.

We draped my old Barbie doll's shimmeriest dresses on the branches, and my fanciest barrettes and bracelets, and some brightly colored socks, and a few shiny toys.

We took turns checking for trouble. It was a pub-

lic park, but we weren't at all sure that this was okay.

"Look!" Lucy shrieked, pointing at my sparkly sunglasses bobbing on a branch that looked like a giant nose.

When we stood back, clutching each other, to view our creation, Lucy burst out laughing so hard that I couldn't understand what she was saying.

"What?" I asked, catching her giggles.

"IZZZZ PERRRTSSSSLEEE HEEEEDIUMPHOUS!" she repeated.

"What?" I cried, trying to pull the laugh cramps out of my face with my hands.

"It's perfectly hideous! The ugliest Christmas tree ever!" Lucy said.

"Maybe if we squint really hard," I said, "until our eyes are almost closed...." Then we both laughed so hard we fell over.

But when Lucy's mom called that night, Lucy took the phone into my parents' room and closed the door. She came out looking glum. At first I thought maybe Lucy's grandma's eighty-one-year-old baby sister in Texas had died. But Lucy said, "No, in fact, she's out of the hospital and doing better, my mom says."

"Well, are you mad at me?" I asked her.

She just said, "No."

"So, what's wrong?" I asked.

Lucy shrugged. "I'm fine," she said. "Really." But she wasn't fine. That was clear.

I wondered if Lucy could still be mad about the library-Ned thing, but I didn't think so.

The phone rang again and my mom got it. In a few minutes she called out, "Marla and Ned, Daddy's on the phone."

Usually Ned knocks everyone and everything out of his way to get to the phone first, but not this time. So I talked to my dad. "My show will be on in a half hour," he reminded me.

I did not ask why he was still in Washington if his segment was all finished and ready for TV. Especially California time. But he must have read my mind because he said that he had been editing up until the last minute.

"And now," he said, "it's an overly white Christmas in Washington. So white, in fact, that the airport is closed."

When I was done talking to him, I yelled for

Ned, but he didn't come, so my mom took her turn. She shooed me away so she could talk mushy. When she was done she called for Ned, but he still didn't come.

"That was Daddy," I said, "but Mom hung up."

"I don't wanna talk to Daddy," Ned said. "I hate Daddy."

My mom, who has X-ray ears for that sort of thing, came swooping into the room. She crouched down next to Ned and launched into one of her helpful lectures. "Now, you don't mean that, Neddy. I think you're just mad at Daddy because he's not here. Daddy loves you and he wishes he could be here, but he has to do his work and now he is caught in a blizzard," and on and on and on....

After the candles and the song I said, "Some party." There's that line in the song, "Let's have a party, we'll all dance the hora...." And there we were, whiny Ned, mopey Lucy, me, my mom, period.

"Now it's parties you want?" my mom asked.

Before I'd even answered, Ned said, "YES!"

"Okay," she said, "so here's something to wear to the party." She gave me an outfit that for once was only one size too big. And she gave Lucy one to match. "Merry Christmas," my mom said.

"Can we really have a party?" I asked.

"Okay," she said again. "The last night of Hanukkah."

Then it was time for the sextuplets. Lucy and I sat on the white leather couch, Ned lay on the white carpet, and my mom leaned against the white wall. My dad's "warm-fuzzy" segment was usually on last, but in honor of Christmas tonight's show was going to be one warm-fuzzy after another. Luckily my dad's segment was first so we didn't have to watch all the other ones.

Actually the Raisins were pretty cute and there were some funny parts, like when one of them was eating his Santa hat and another almost pulled the tree down on her head and all six of them burst into horrified tears at the sight of their father dressed as Santa Claus.

Then my mom took Ned, kicking and screaming, off for his bath, and Lucy and I watched an old Christmas movie.

We both cried at the end, but Lucy kept crying.

My mom came in and saw Lucy crying and me sitting like a lump. She sat between us and put her arms around Lucy.

"Even grown-ups get sad being away from their families on Christmas Eve," my mom said. "Holidays are powerful family stuff."

I was glad to hear that my mom didn't think that Lucy's bad mood was about me.

But my mom's helpful lecture went on from there, about Lucy's feelings being natural, and how Christmas is a time to be with loved ones and to appreciate family and so on. . . .

Lucy stopped crying and pretty soon started looking bored and restless. Good, I thought, now we can go back to normal. And we did.

Sometime in the middle of the night I woke up and heard the pit-pit-pit of Ned's bare feet on the wood floor. Next I saw his face peering over the edge of my bed.

"Can I come in?" Ned asked.

"Go to Mommy, Neddy," I whispered, but he said, "No."

I looked closer and saw that he was weepy. I lifted the blanket so he could crawl in, and I asked him what was the matter.

"Daddy," Ned said.

I figured that he felt guilty for not talking to our dad on the phone, so I said, "You'll talk to him tomorrow."

"Daddy's caught by a wizard," Ned said, and started crying for real.

"You just had a bad dream, a nightmare," I said.

"Mommy said so!" he insisted. "Do you think Superman will come?"

I was so tired, and Ned was so sad. Then it came to me. "Daddy's caught in a *blizzard*, not caught by a *wizard*!" I said. "A blizzard is a snowstorm. Remember when we were at Bubbi and Poppa's in Michigan and there was a lot of snow? That's a blizzard. His plane just can't take off."

We must have awakened Lucy, because her fuzzy voice came from the other bed. "And he's not caught outside in the blizzard. He's inside a nice warm hotel," she said, "in a nice warm bed."

"Superman won't come?" Ned asked.

"Superman is sleeping," I said, "like Daddy." Ned

snuggled up with me and was snoring in no time.

"See?" Lucy whispered. "No one ever comes to me with their lizards and gizzards."

"You'd be a wonderful big sister," I said.

"Shhhhh!" she said. "You'll wake him."

CHAPTER
·········· 8 ··········

On Christmas morning Lucy and I packed a picnic and told my mom we'd take Ned with us to the park if she promised to come and get him in one hour *exactly*.

We took turns pulling him in the wagon. When Ned waved and said, "Hi, Daddy," to a jet passing overhead, Lucy looked sorry for him.

"It's okay," I told her. "Ned does that even when my dad is standing right next to him."

We had taken down all our glitter-litter the day before, but when we got back to our secret tree we did find one stray Barbie shoe.

Lucy and I were being twin sisters in the jungle and Ned was our pet lion cub. We were hunting for bugs and snakes to eat. Ned was roaring at the joggers and other jungle creatures, as lion cubs do.

When he roared at one guy who was walking a huge gray dog, the dog lunged, barking furiously, and scared the bejeebees out of Ned. He started to cry and scream.

Luckily my mom kept her promise and showed up just then. After they were gone, Lucy and I lay down on a blanket to watch clouds.

Lucy seemed her old self again, but I said, "Is my mom right that you miss your family more than you usually would because it's Christmas?"

"Hmmmm," Lucy said.

"Remember last year when my dad started going to Washington for the Raisins, and he didn't make it home for my birthday?" I asked. "Is it like that?"

Lucy rolled over and looked at me. "You never told me that you were mad or sad or anything," she said.

"I was."

Lucy rolled back over and we watched three little wispy clouds blend into each other.

"You better be careful not to make Hanukkah too good," Lucy said, "or you'll miss it when you can't have it."

"Yeah," I agreed. "Maybe we should make sure we always have a really bad time doing everything, so we never miss anything."

"Sounds fun," Lucy giggled.

When we got home, my mom was on the phone inviting people to the party. First she invited the few Jewish people she knows here. Then she said, "What the heck," and invited the rest of the people she knows.

Lucy and I could hear her from my room, where we were drawing pictures.

"Queen Marla," we heard her say, "has decreed that we gather to celebrate the Festival of Lights." On another call she said, "On behalf of our own Miss Marla, I summon you to honor the rededication of the Temple of the Maccabees."

I was just about to say that I thought my mom was terminally embarrassing when Lucy said, "Your mom is the greatest."

"You're kidding, right?" I asked.

Lucy and I stared at each other, our faces a mirror image of amazement with her blue eyes as stumped as my brown ones.

"But *your* mom is so normal!" I said.

73
◆

"You mean boring," Lucy said.

We thought about it awhile, then agreed that if we mushed the two moms together into one, everything would be better.

"Like if I could have your long hair," Lucy said. I tried to picture my heavy dark hair on her.

"But your blue eyes, and Yaz's everything..." I said. Then, looking over at Lucy's drawing of a horse, I added, "And your artistic talent."

"Plus your Rollerblading," she said, "and your bedroom, and—"

I interrupted her. "My bedroom? It's just totally boring white, like every other room in this dumb house. Your room has all that ancient, dark, probably haunted furniture. I have the world's dullest venetian blinds—white, of course. Your room has those heavy curtains like in a castle."

"You forgot one other thing my room has," Lucy said. "KATE!"

"But it must be a blast sharing with her!" I said, imagining one lifelong sleep-over. "I mean, when she's not being a porcupine."

"You're kidding, right?" Lucy said. And there we were, mirrors of amazement again.

"Lucy?" I said, suddenly getting up my nerve. "Can I tell you something really terrible?"

"What?" she asked.

"Do you promise not to hate me?" I asked, feeling my face heat up.

"Of course I won't hate you," said Lucy.

I decided to get it over with really fast. "Last year I stole an ornament off your mom's Christmas tree and threw it out," I blurted.

Lucy laughed. "No wonder we're best friends!"

"Why are you laughing?" I said.

Lucy laughed some more, then said, "Want to hear mine?"

"Hear your what?" I asked.

"When Ned was a baby and I wanted a baby in my house so badly—and you guys had all those sweet little things...tiny booties and soft little crib toys and all, remember?"

"Yes," I said.

"I took a rattle with a yellow lamb on it."

"You're kidding!" I said, feeling happier than I'd been in a year. "Do you still have it?"

"I was so afraid you'd see it in my drawer that after a while, I threw it away too!" Lucy shrieked.

75
◆

And we both flew into hysterics.

Before we lit the candles for the seventh night, Mom said, "I thought making Hanukkah was an old-lady thing. Bubbi made Hanukkah, Auntie Eva made Hanukkah. But I just did the math, and those old ladies were slinging latkes when they were younger than I am now. So either I'm an old lady or they weren't."

Later that night my dad called to say he really, really, really was on his way home, but there were some problems with connecting flights or something. I didn't know. I didn't care. I only knew he wasn't home.

"Ned isn't going to like it one bit if my dad misses the party," I told Lucy.

It was Lucy's and my last night together. We looked through that library book on the Jewish holidays and read the Hanukkah part.

"Yeech!" I said. "I'm glad we didn't live back then. I wouldn't have the courage to hide in caves and fight the army and stuff."

"I bet you would," Lucy said. "The story would be 'Marla Feinstein and the Maccabees.'"

"Would you come with me?" I asked. "Into the caves?"

"You bet!" Lucy said.

CHAPTER

•••••••• 9 ••••••••

When I woke up the next morning my dad was home, asleep in bed. I couldn't keep Ned from pounding him awake. Actually I didn't really try. My dad was zonked, he said, "from swimming upstream like a salmon" to get home to us. He swooped me up in his arms as if I were as small as Ned, and he gave me one big, scratchy kiss for each day he had been gone. He needed a shave.

Dad opened his eyes wide. "Red-eye, see?" he said to Ned. "Like Cookie the rat." Then he went back to bed. It was okay that he was asleep—he was home.

We all tiptoed out of the house, me, Lucy, my mom, and Ned, and went to the market to buy the stuff for our party. I knew that probably no one in the store thought Lucy and I were twin sisters, but I also knew it was my last chance to feel like we were.

Lucy's family came to pick her up just before

lunch. She squeezed into the car with them as I watched from the porch. It wasn't like she was *leaving* leaving. They were just going four-and-a-half blocks away, so why was I sad?

Lucy poked her head out the car window and yelled: "We'll all be back later for the party!" So I guessed she'd invited them first thing, after hello. Lots of hands came shooting out of the windows to wave, and they sped off.

My mom spent hours cleaning the toilets and hissing at us whenever we touched *anything*. She couldn't really yell or she'd wake my dad.

"Daddy's home," Ned would announce every few minutes to me or my mom, as if we didn't know. I heard him tell his stuffed animals too.

In the car on our way back to the market my mom said, "You know, the light of the oil lamp was never supposed to go out once it was lit. But folks were so busy redecorating the Temple and washing the toilets, it took eight days to remember to buy more oil."

I made a face at her.

"No, you're right, maybe the grocery store was an eight-day, round-trip, donkey ride from the Temple."

"MOM!"

"Well, Miss Marla, why do you think it had to last eight days? To give them time to dig an oil well?"

"Maybe it took that long to squeeze enough oil out of the olives, or something," I said.

"We will look it up," my mom said, "next Hanukkah."

"Daddy's home?" Ned asked, looking scared.

"Yup. He's home," my mom said, taking her hand off the steering wheel to pat Ned's foot in the car-seat.

She unpacked the groceries from our second trip to the market, then called her friend Sue to pick up sour cream on her way over.

"Good thing it's not a long donkey ride to the store," I said.

Ned and I made Hanukkah decorations for the windows as best we could without making my mom totally hysterical about the mess. Ned isn't much of an artist. He called one scribble a dreidel and one a latke, but they looked pretty much the same to me. I cut out a menorah and carefully colored each candle in a different pattern. It wasn't as nice as Lucy would have made it, but it was pretty darn good.

About an hour before the party my dad came shuffling out of his bedroom with droopy shoulders and a saggy face. But when he saw our art taped up on the windows, he lit up like a menorah.

People started coming around 4:30. I heard our neighbor Doreen say that she had a hard time convincing her son Sean that it was okay to come. He didn't think they should because it wasn't their holiday.

Then Lucy and her entire family, even Grandma, were at the door. Lucy and I were both wearing the outfits my mom had given us. Hers looked just as goofy on her as mine did on me.

Lucy had brought the blue-and-white decoration that she'd made at school the day we had that sub. I taped her sky with animal clouds up on the window with my menorah art and Ned's dreidel and latke squiggles.

I heard Lucy's mom telling my dad that they had all watched his sextuplet Christmas show in their hotel room in Texas, and that they'd loved it. Lucy's mom asked all the usual questions about how the parents cope with so many toddlers. And my dad gave his usual answers about how they do their best and find joy where they can.

Everyone just ran around for a while. Ned's friends were especially nutso—but not Ned. He spent the entire Hanukkah party either riding on my dad's shoulders or practically Velcroed to his leg.

We lit the full menorah. My dad turned out the lights and everybody got quiet because it was so pretty. Joe from the deli said the blessing of the Hanukkah candles in Hebrew.

Then everyone who knew the words sang "Oh Hanukkah," and it sounded great. There was me and my mom and my dad with his big voice, and Ned sort of sang, and Lucy and Joe and Joe's Wife, whose name turned out to be Rose. But boy, was I surprised when I noticed Lucy's sister Yaz singing along too! Lucy must have taught it to her that very day.

Next my mom asked me if I would like to tell the story of Hanukkah to everyone—"Marla's version," she said—and I did.

"Long ago and far away," I began, "a king named Antiochus declared it a crime to be Jewish. It was

against the law to pray to just one God. Lots of Jewish people started bowing and praying to the king's Greek gods and acting just like everyone else.

"But some Jews disobeyed the king and secretly kept to their old ways and beliefs. The king hated that. He sent some soldiers to put up an idol in the Temple and make a Jew sacrifice a pig to it. A few Jews revolted and fought the soldiers.

"Then the king was really mad, so he sent more soldiers. A man named Mattathias led his sons and a small band of Jews to live in caves in the hills, where he taught them to fight. After a year Mattathias died and his son Judah took over. His nickname was Maccabee, and the whole band of warrior Jews was soon called the Maccabees. They were way outnumbered by the bigger and bigger armies that the king sent to kill them, but the Maccabees kept winning.

"The king was furious. For the last battle he sent fighting elephants and his very best soldiers. But the Maccabees fought so fiercely that, against all odds, the king's soldiers retreated and the war was over.

"The Maccabees went home to their village to celebrate and found that their Temple had been destroyed."

"Bummer," said Yaz.

I told everyone about the rebuilding of the Temple and the miracle of the oil lasting eight nights and that's why we light candles for eight nights.

Then I said that before vacation my teacher had made me make a blue-and-white candle when all the rest of the class was making red-and-green ones.

"None of my other teachers before had ever singled me out as the only Jewish kid in class. But the story of Hanukkah makes me think Mrs. Guyer was sort of right—I shouldn't have to make red-and-green decorations all the time just because everyone else is. I am me—blue and white."

"Bravo!" my dad yelled, and everyone clapped and cheered for me. My mom looked teary.

"I leave town for a few days," my dad said, "and my kid turns the whole family into characters in a warm-fuzzy Hanukkah segment."

"Are we as heartwarming as the sextuplets in Santa hats?" I asked.

"You have a promising future in television," my dad said, winking.

My mom walked by just then and said, "God forbid!"

Later almost everyone danced! My mom led the dancers in a chain, snaking through the kitchen and living room with the hora tape at full volume. And we played dreidel with kids calling out the letters so loud that the grown-ups all left the room.

Sean, the neighbor kid who hadn't wanted to come in the first place, told me he didn't want a latke. Then he tried one when everyone else did. "It's just hash browns!" he said, and had seconds.

Everyone brought a grab-bag gift for a kid. My mom had told them that the gifts were to be cheap. A token. But some people didn't listen and I got one of the gifts those people brought. Forty-eight Magic Markers and two huge pads of paper. When no one was looking, I traded it with Lucy for the jigsaw puzzle she'd gotten. Lucy promised to draw me a picture of my Hanukkah party, using all forty-eight colors.

I was walking Lucy and her family to the door when Yaz turned to me and said, "This was fun. I can't believe we all fell for your pathetic story about how dreary Hanukkah is!"

"Well, it wasn't always like this," I laughed.

When everyone was gone but us, and my mom was done complaining about the mess, and sleeping Ned had been peeled off Dad's shoulder and put to bed, my parents came into my room.

"Mom tells me this was all your doing," my dad said. "The party, the hora, everything.... So you're probably going to do all the dishes and cleaning up yourself too, right?"

My mom rolled her eyes at him, so he said, "Just kidding."

Mom gave me a hug, saying, "You are really something else, Miss Marla. I'm very lucky to have a daughter like you ... even if you did turn me into my old Auntie Eva." She hugged me again and she didn't let go for a long, long time.

Hanukkah was over.

The next morning my mom said, "Now, does anybody want to run out and get some Christmas lights and ornaments for next year? This is the perfect time for sales."

"I do!" Ned said. "Can we *really*?"

"It's up to Marla," said Mom.

I knew it was a test, but I also knew it was my

only chance to have a tree, ornaments, colored lights. … I tried to picture our house all decorated like Lucy's. Our white-on-white living room with cotton clouds on the mantel, red candles, and stockings? Even in my mind it didn't fit right.

So it didn't take me *that* long to say, "Nah, we're Jewish."

My mom gave me the thumbs-up sign, but Ned socked me. He has a lot to learn. Really.